The Berenstain Bears® at the GIANT MALL

Stan & Jan Berenstain

A GOLDEN BOOK • NEW YORK
Western Publishing Company, Inc., Racine, Wisconsin 53404

Here we go!

We're on our way!

We're going
to the mall today!

Are we almost there,
Papa Bear?

Yes, my dear.
We're almost there.

There it is,
the giant mall,
with its flying flags
and towers tall.

Here's something else
this mall has got—
one humongous
parking lot.

Now we're in
the giant mall,
with its giant
entrance hall.

Look! A giant
escalator.
We'll try it out
a little later!

With stores and shops
of every kind,
there is no telling
what we'll find
in this amazing
giant mall!

A wedding dress,

a soccer ball.

Picture frames,

tables, chairs,

clothes for big
and little bears.

10

Tents and other
stuff for camp,

a birthday card
for Grizzly Gramp.

Kitchen things,

jewelry,

books,

a police bear watching
out for crooks.

Cookie counters,

carts of flowers.

We could shop
for hours and hours!

And hours and hours
and hours and hours!

Let's do some shopping

for ourselves.

We need some things.

Let's search the shelves.

These overalls look
just Pa's size.
And they're the kind
he always buys.

Ma could use

a brand-new hat.

A perfect fit.

Now fancy that!

Brother needs
some balsa wood.
His model planes
are very good!

What shall we buy
for Sister Bear?
An extra hair bow
for her hair!

HAIR
BOW

Do you like yellow,
green, or blue?
They all would look
18   so nice on you.

A new bow would
be nice, I think.
But if you don't mind,
I'll stay with pink.

Bears come here
from everywhere.

They come to shop,

they come to stare.

They come to jog,

they come to eat,

they come to stroll,

they come to meet.

Teenagers come to hang around.

Young cubs are at the Lost and Found.

FOUND

LOST CUB PLACE

We see our neighbor,

Mr. Brown.

We go up

as he goes down.

Pa is lost!

Where's Papa Bear?

We cannot find him

24 anywhere!

We find him at
the lost cub place,
an embarrassed look
upon his face.

LOST
CUB
PLACE

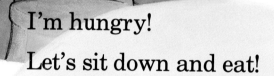

I'm hungry!

Let's sit down and eat!

Good! Let's rest
our tired feet.

We really like
this giant mall,
with its bears and stores
from wall to wall.

27

Yes, my dears,

I do agree.

But it's time to leave.

Please follow me.

Will we find
our car, or not,
in this humongous
parking lot?

Yes, we'll find it in this lot.
Mama Bear wrote down
the spot!

D3

D1

C5

C4

29

Good-bye! Good-bye,
you giant mall!
With your bears and stores
from wall to wall,

with your giant
entrance hall,
your flying flags
and towers tall.

GIANT
MALL

We'll be back!

We can't say when.

But count on it:

We will visit you again.